Little Sima and the Giant Bowl

A Chinese Folktale

Adapted by ZHI QU

Illustrated by LIN WANG

On My Own

FOLKLORE

M Millbrook Press/Minneapolis

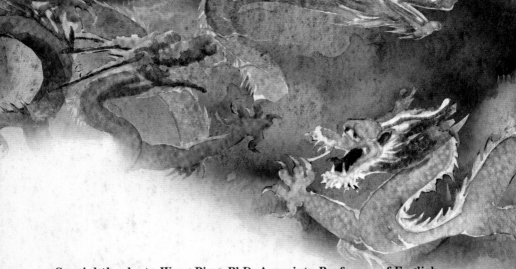

Special thanks to Wang Ping, PhD, Associate Professor of English, Macalester College, for serving as a consultant on this title

Text copyright © 2009 by Zhi Qu
Illustrations copyright © 2009 by Lerner Publishing Group, Inc.

Millbrook Press
A division of Lerner Publishing Group, Inc.
241 First Avenue North
Minneapolis, MN 55401 U.S.A.

Website address: www.lernerbooks.com

Library of Congress Cataloging-in-Publication Data

Qu, Zhi.
    Little sima and the giant bowl : a Chinese folktale / by Zhi Qu ; illustrated by Lin Wang.
        p.   cm. — (On my own folklore)
    ISBN: 978–0–8225–7620–4 (lib. bdg. : alk. paper)
    1. Tales—China. 2. Folklore–China. I. Wang, Lin. II. Title.
GR335.Q32 2009
398.20951—dc22   2007014247

Manufactured in the United States of America
1 2 3 4 5 6 – DP – 14 13 12 11 10 09

To the memory of my uncle Zhao Qirui —Z.Q.

For my daughter, Megan, and my sons, Willson and Nicholas
—L.W.

Legend has it that Little Sima
was a lucky child.
He lived in a beautiful village
on the banks of a great river.
He had all the love, friendship,
and fun a boy could wish for.
As a young child, Little Sima read
many books and knew many stories.
He liked to watch dragons
weave clouds in the sky.
And he liked to hear stories
about his ancestors.
Little Sima especially liked
hearing about the life
of his great-great-grandfather.

Great-great-grandfather Sima had
a happy life, just as Little Sima had.
He lived in the same beautiful village.
Just like Little Sima,
Great-great-grandfather loved to watch
a dragon weave clouds in the sky.

The great dragon took threads
of white dew and wove clouds
of different patterns.
Sometimes rain would fall
from these clouds.
And sometimes it would be snow.

But one winter day, the great dragon
that wove clouds for the village
grew tired of his job.
He turned his back on his duty.
Chinese dragons had to live where
there was plenty of water,
in clouds or in rivers or lakes.
So the dragon came down from the skies
to live in the river that ran past
the village.
He became known as the black dragon
to all who lived in the village.

Because no one was weaving clouds
in the village sky, the village had no rain.
The earth became dry.
The river grew shallow.

The shallow water in the river
annoyed the black dragon.
In anger, he rose from the river
to breathe out fire every year.

The fire burned houses and plants
near the river.
It charred the trees.
It turned the once-green riverbanks
into a wasteland.
Worst of all,
after the dragon breathed out fire,
he would become exhausted.
So he would swallow a whole well
of water to regain his strength.
Soon, all the wells in the village
were dry.

The village became poorer and bleaker
each year.
For fear of the black dragon,
the families all kept their doors bolted.
The streets became empty.

No laughter was heard.

No children played outside.

Without rain, the crops could not grow.

The animals starved.

Food and drinking water became scarce.

The whole village suffered
these hardships for one hundred years.
Yet the Simas remained hardworking, kind,
and hopeful for a better life.
One hundred years after
the black dragon left the skies,
Little Sima was born.
The family embraced their baby child
with joy and sorrow.
How would he survive?

One day at dusk, an old man dressed
in rags came to beg at the Simas' door.
He was so old and fragile
that he had to lean on a stick.
Could he survive the chill of the night
on the street?
Little Sima's parents were kind people,
so they invited the old man
into their house.
They shared their meager supper
of porridge with him.
Porridge was the only food
they had eaten for a month.
After supper, Little Sima's father
put up a bed so the old man
could rest for the night.

When Little Sima's parents woke up
the next morning, they found
the old man meditating on a straw mat.
He looked stronger after a night's sleep.
He thanked the Simas for saving his life,
"the life of an old beggar," as he said.
He told them, "Before I leave this world,
I want to give you my only earthly
possession.
It is a fish *gang*.
It will turn your luck around and make
your family prosper."
Then he warned, "You must take good
care of this *gang*.
Its magic power will end if it is broken."
Little Sima's parents listened
to their guest in bewilderment.

Before they could thank him for the gift,
the old man vanished
into the morning dew.
Little Sima's parents realized
that their guest was a wizard in disguise.
They walked outside.
There they found a giant porcelain bowl
standing in the courtyard
under their old linden tree.
It was an amazing *gang*, glazed with nine
blue dragons around the outside.

Inside, it was glazed
with beautiful goldfish.
Little Sima's parents knew that
this was the gift of the Great Wizard.
They gathered in front of the *gang*.
They thanked their mysterious guest
for this wonderful gift.

At noon that day, the villagers saw
nine blue dragons appear in the sky.
The dragons began to weave clouds
above the village.
Lightning pierced the sky.
Thunder crashed.

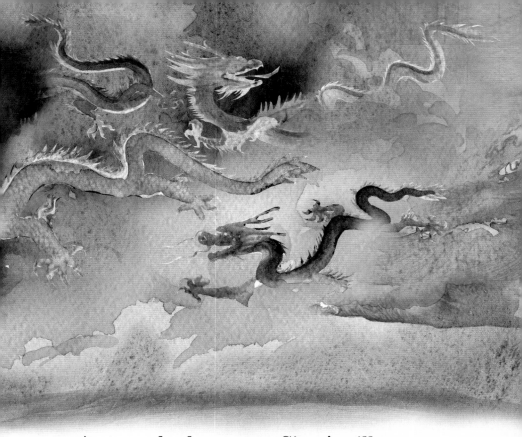

A storm had come to Sima's village
for the first time in one hundred years.
It rained the whole afternoon,
the whole evening, and the whole night.
The villagers came out of their homes.
They danced and laughed in the rain.
Their hearts were filled with joy.

From then on, the mindful blue
dragons saw to it that Sima's village
had enough rain.
Trees, flowers, and grass began
to cover the land.
Clear water filled the wells
and the river.

Children played outside.
The village was full of life again.
The unfaithful black dragon
retreated to the deepest part
of the river in disgust.

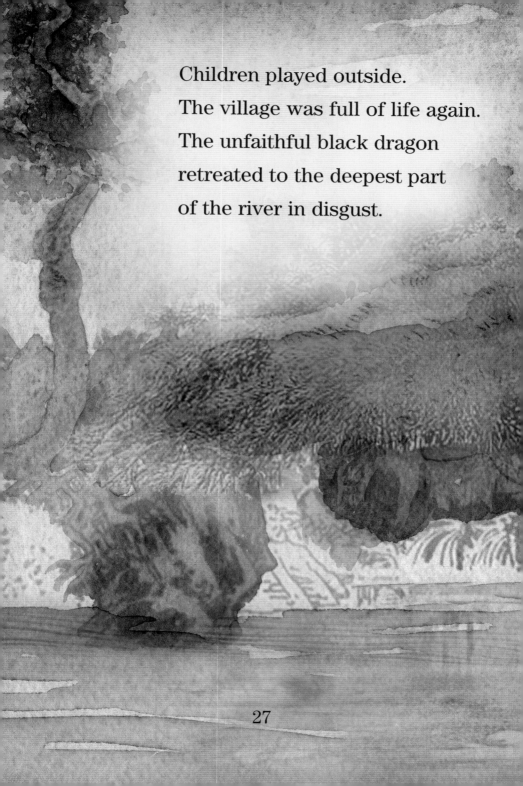

In eight years, the Sima family
became prosperous again.
They were so grateful
for the Great Wizard that they treasured
the *gang* above everything else.
To adorn the *gang*, they filled it
with the most beautiful goldfish.
They planted firs and flowers nearby.
Wealthy as they were, the Simas
were still kind, hard working, and good.
They hoped their little boy would grow
up to be a brave and clever young man.

Little Sima never disappointed
his parents.
He studied hard and was always
obedient and respectful.
He knew that it was the Great Wizard
who had brought about
his family's wealth and comfort.
He loved sitting under the linden tree
to read or to admire the *gang*.
Sometimes he would imagine that
the Great Wizard was looking down
from the heavens to watch over him
and his family.

When the weather was nice, Little Sima
played outside with his friends.
One day, a group of children came
to play with Little Sima
in his family's courtyard.

The children talked about the *gang*.
They wanted to measure how fat it was.
Five boys stretched out their arms
to go around it.
"What a big beautiful *gang!*" the children
exclaimed.

They wanted to see the goldfish,

but they couldn't.

The *gang* was too tall.

"I've got a way,"

said one of the youngest boys.

He climbed the linden tree.

He sat on a branch above the *gang*.

"I can see the goldfish!"

he shouted to his friends.

Barely a second after the words

had left his mouth, the branch broke.

Splash!

The boy had fallen into the giant *gang*.

The children were startled.

Then they panicked.

The boy would certainly drown

if they did not do anything.

But they did not know what to do.

"Help! Help!" the children shouted.
But Little Sima's parents were not home.
No one could hear them.
Some children ran out of the courtyard
to look for other grown-ups.

Little Sima did not call or run.

He was calm.

He knew that he had to think fast

to save his friend's life.

He took a big stone from a flower bed.

But he hesitated.

Should he be disrespectful

of the Great Wizard?

Would his parents blame him

for breaking this treasure?

Little Sima had no more time to think.

His friend was gasping out words

for help.

He lifted the stone

and smashed it hard against the *gang*.

The *gang* did not break, but Little Sima

felt an awful pain himself.

His heart was pounding fast.
Then he smashed the stone
against the *gang* again, even harder.
The *gang* began to crack.

At the third stroke, the *gang* broke.

Water poured out.

Little Sima's friend was saved.

Just then, Little Sima's parents
returned home.
His mother rushed into the courtyard.
Little Sima was afraid that she would be
angry with him for breaking
the family's treasure.
Before he could explain, his mother said,
"My son, you did the right thing."
She patted Little Sima on the back.
"Remember, a life is always far more
precious than anything else," she said.

For months, the villagers waited to see
if the black dragon would return.
But there was no sign of him.
Then on a clear day, they saw the nine blue
dragons come out in the sky again.
They began to weave rain clouds.

Lightning pierced the sky.

Thunder crashed.

Rain began to fall.

Little Sima and his mother ran
into the courtyard to see the *gang*.

They found the cracks in it were gone.

It was as beautiful as it had ever been.

Afterword

This folktale is about a real person, Sima Guang. Sima Guang lived from 1019 to 1086 in China, during the Song dynasty. He was very bright and hard working. He studied hard and received the highest academic degree, *jinshi*, at the age of 19. As an adult, he served as a government official similar to the secretary of state. Sima Guang wrote a remarkable book on Chinese history called *Zizhi Tongjian*, which means "A Mirror for Good Governance." Most people in China still read *Zizhi Tongjian*.

The story that Sima Guang broke the *gang* to save his friend's life has become a folktale. For hundreds of years, parents have told their children the story. Like all folktales, this tale is told to teach a lesson. Little Sima is a role model of heroism for children. He went against the rules and looked inside himself to find the right answer. As in folktales all over the world, the hero finds truth by searching himself.

Dragons appear in many Chinese folktales. They are powerful creatures that can fly and swim. They can change people's lives. Dragons often represent forces that people cannot control, such as storms, drought, earthquakes, or floods.

Sima Guang's name written in Chinese characters looks like this: 司马光

Glossary

ancestors: members of a person's family who lived long ago

bewilderment: confusion

courtyard: an outdoor space surrounded by walls

dew: water droplets

fir: a type of evergreen tree

fragile: easily broken

hardship: something that causes suffering

hesitate: to pause or delay for a moment

gang **(GAHNG):** a porcelain bowl

meager: not enough

meditate: to focus one's thoughts

porcelain: a type of fine pottery; also called china

porridge: a soft food made of boiled grains, like oatmeal or grits

precious: of great value

prosperous: marked by success

scarce: hard to find

well: a hole in the ground that is a source of freshwater

Further Reading and Websites

Books

Krach, Maywan Shen. *D Is for Doufu: An Alphabet Book of Chinese Culture*. Arcadia, CA: Shen's Books, 1997. This book uses 46 Chinese characters to introduce Chinese history and customs. Each character is accompanied by a written image and an explanation of the spoken Mandarin language.

Louie, Belinda. *Learning Chinese: Through Stories and Activities*. Bothell, WA: Book Publishers Network, 2007. The stories in this bilingual book, which includes the tale of Little Sima, are printed in English and Chinese. The book also presents a number of Chinese games and activities.

Ping, Wang. *The Dragon Emperor: A Chinese Folktale*. Minneapolis: Millbrook Press, 2007. This Chinese folktale introduces dragon-emperor Ying Long and his battles against the demon rebel Chi You.

Simonds, Nina. *Moonbeams, Dumplings & Dragon Boats: A Treasury of Chinese Holiday Tales, Activities & Recipes*. San Diego: Harcourt, 2002. This book showcases five holidays—Chinese New Year, the Lantern Festival, Qing Ming, the Dragon Boat Festival, and the Mid-Autumn Moon Festival—through a history of the holiday, and a description of its customs, legends, recipes, and games.

Yip, Mingmei. *Chinese Children's Favorite Stories*. Boston: Tuttle Publishing, 2004. Most of these 13 "thousand-year-old" stories have traditional Chinese elements such as dragons and the impish monkey king.

Zemlicka, Shannon. *Colors of China*. Minneapolis: Carolrhoda Books, 2001. Each color presented gives information about the history, physical features, or culture of China.

Websites

Chinese Dragons

http://www.crystalinks.com/chinadragons.html

http://library.thinkquest.org/CR0215373/

These two websites tell about Chinese dragons, what they symbolize in Chinese folktales, and how they are different from Western dragons.

Stories from Around the World: Sima Guang

http://www.midtesol.org/ClassProjects/project1/story4e.htm

This class project tells the story of Sima Guang rescuing his friend.